Junkyard TOUGH

A "TAIL" OF BRAVERY

By Jenny Baertsch

Illustrated & Designed by Sara Pientok

BAERTSCH BOOKS

Winona, Minnesota

Published by Baertsch Books, Winona, Minnesota. Baertsch Books name
and associated logos are trademarks of Baertsch Books. For more information
regarding the author and publisher, visit www.BaertschBooks.com.

ISBN 978-0-578-97804-8

First edition printed October 2021

Printed in the U.S.A. by Mediascope, Inc., Winona, Minnesota

For Tessa and Chase.

Anything is possible with hard work and bravery.

For Boots.

A small kitten with a big story.

Junkyard Tough

A "Tail" of Bravery

Contents

1
Junkyard Morning

When you live in a junkyard, you need to be tough.

That's what Mama Cat always told him. Her little kitten spent his nights sleeping in an old, worn-out work boot. And that's why she named him "Boots."

Boots had to be a tough cat. Junkyards were NOT for scaredy-cats. They were loud, dirty places and home to many animals that would eat just about anything—even cats!

During his junkyard adventures, Boots saw gigantic birds, hungry raccoons, and rats that were bigger than he was. Most mornings he woke to the sound of a truck picking up trash for the landfill.

But he never felt scared. No way! Boots was junkyard tough, just like Mama Cat always told him to be.

One summer morning, Boots woke up in his boot, yawned, and stretched in the sun.

What a beautiful day in the junkyard! he thought.

"Good morning, Boots," Mama Cat said. "Will you be junkyard tough and hunt for our breakfast? You're such a great hunter!"

"Yes, Mama!" Boots answered proudly.

Boots liked hunting for food. The junkyard had a menu full of choices!

What should we eat today? Pizza crust from the trash? Maybe a tasty mouse?

His stomach growled at the thought of a mouse—and as luck would have it—he saw movement in the trash pile.

"A MOUSE!" Boots shouted with excitement. "BREAKFAST TIME!"

Boots pounced into action, running and chasing the mouse past the trash pile, through the old cars, and all the way to the junkyard office.

But the chase quickly ended when the mouse escaped through a small hole in the bottom of the office building.

Boots looked up at the building. *I've never been this close before.*

The junkyard office was where "people" worked. Since he was still a young kitten, Boots was never this close to people before. He and Mama Cat always stayed out of sight.

Curious about his discovery, Boots tip-toed past the office door, jumped up on a ledge, and peeked in the open window.

What a busy place! he thought. Paper was stacked on every desk, and people walked around in different directions.

A loud *RING!* from a phone startled Boots. But before he could run away, someone lifted him off the window ledge.

2
A New Friend

"**H**ey there, little buddy," a man's voice said softly as he picked up Boots.

It was Mr. Meowington, the junkyard office manager. He pulled Boots in through the open window and set him on his desk.

Boots cautiously looked around. He noticed a picture frame on the desk.

They must be the man's family, he thought as he admired the group of smiling people in the picture.

A woman sat next to Mr. Meowington on a bench, while a young girl and boy were on the ground next to a dog with its tongue hanging out!

They look happy together! Even though Boots had Mama Cat in the junkyard, he couldn't help but wonder what it would feel like to be part of a big family.

"The junkyard is a loud place. You're a brave kitten!" Mr. Meowington said to Boots. "Are you hungry?"

Boots wondered, *What does brave mean? Am I brave when I'm hungry?* Since the mouse escaped, he hadn't eaten any breakfast, and he was starving!

While Boots thought about what brave meant, Mr. Meowington found a cold french fry from yesterday's lunch and held it in front of Boots.

"Go on, take it," Mr. Meowington encouraged. "You'll like it. I promise!"

Boots carefully took the fry in his mouth. It was delicious! He gobbled it up, then looked up at his new friend.

"More?" Mr. Meowington asked as he laughed and put more fries in front of Boots.

After Boots finished eating, Mr. Meowington bundled a yellow t-shirt on his desk to make a comfy bed. Boots laid on the soft shirt with his belly full of day-old fries. He never felt so comfortable!

His old, worn-out work boot bed was becoming a memory. *RING!* went the phone, but this time it didn't scare Boots.

He was fast asleep next to the picture frame.

When he opened his eyes, Boots didn't recognize his surroundings.

Am I dreaming?

He blinked the sleep from his eyes, hoping to see the picture frame, but instead he saw strange, brown walls. All he recognized was the yellow shirt.

Boots felt scared. His heart beat faster and faster in his chest. He stood up, looked up, and was relieved to find his new friend's face smiling above.

"Time to go home, little buddy," Mr. Meowington whispered.

3
A Big Family

The brown floor started moving. Boots tried to stay standing but fell onto the yellow shirt. The brown walls were moving, too.

He was being carried in a cardboard box!

Boots heard Mr. Meowington whistling, then a *CREAK!* when the car door opened, and a *SLAM!* when it closed.

Am I inside the trash truck? he wondered.

His box stopped moving. The engine started, and the ride felt bumpy with many stops and turns. Boots laid on the shirt to keep his balance, wondering when—and where—the wild ride would end!

Boots felt relieved when the engine finally shut off. The car door creaked open, and his box started moving again.

Where am I? he asked himself.

"KITTTTTTTY!" a young voice squealed.

Panicked, Boots looked up to see a girl reaching into his box. It was the young girl from Mr. Meowington's picture frame.

He ran to the corner of the box, trying to escape, but her small hands reached in and picked him up.

Boots heard another young voice and saw it was a boy.

"Can we keep him?" the boy asked sweetly.

"As long as you help care for him," a woman's voice answered. It was the woman from the family picture.

"Having a pet is a big responsibility," Mrs. Meowington told the kids as she stood next to her husband, Mr. Meowington.

The girl hugged Boots tightly.

"Be careful!" Mrs. Meowington said sharply. "He's a small kitten, and we need to be very gentle!"

The girl put Boots on the floor, giving the family its first look at his fuzzy body. He was gray from head-to-tail, except for white hair on his chest, belly, and under his nose.

And most notably—all four of his feet were white.

"His white feet look like white boots!" Mrs. Meowington said while laughing. "I have the perfect name. Boots Meowington, welcome to our family!"

Boots smiled. *I'm part of a big family!*

It didn't take long for Boots to settle in with the Meowington family. He went from hunting for food every morning to being served a bowl of cat food twice a day. And he no longer slept in a boot, because the Meowingtons had plenty of comfy blankets.

Boots laid down for a nap, thinking about how lucky he was to be inside.

What could go wrong?

4
Feeling Scared

"**B**ARK! BARK!"

Startled by the noise, Boots jumped four feet in the air, landed on his white feet, and ran to find a hiding spot.

The *BARK!* noise was chasing him, getting closer and closer. Boots never heard barking in the junkyard!

He felt scared and hid behind a toy fire truck under the boy's bed.

The fire truck suddenly moved. But before Boots could run away, the boy sat down in front of him.

"Don't be scared, Boots," the boy said. "That's just our dog. She's very kind. Be brave and come out!"

There was that word again: *brave*. Boots remembered how Mr. Meowington called him brave for living in the loud junkyard.

Boots cautiously crawled to the boy, who picked him up and put him face-to-face with the dog. Boots crouched down in fear, expecting to hear another *BARK!* or to find himself in the dog's mouth!

But to his surprise, the dog licked him on the face.

"She likes you!" the boy exclaimed. "Being brave paid off!"

And so it did. Boots and the dog became friends, chasing each other around the house and taking naps together in the sun.

One day, Boots and the dog shared a drink from the water bowl, when to their surprise:

VROOM! VROOM!

This time, Boots jumped FIVE feet in the air, landed on his white feet, and ran to find a hiding spot. Feeling scared, he scurried into a closet, trembling while he hid behind a pair of work boots.

When you live in a junkyard, you need to be tough, Boots remembered, but he wasn't in the junkyard anymore. Then he thought of Mama Cat and how much he missed her.

The *VROOM!* noise was getting louder, then suddenly stopped. With caution, Boots peeked around a boot and found Mrs. Meowington kneeling in front of him.

"Don't be scared," she whispered calmly. "Be brave and come out!"

There was that word again. *Whenever I'm feeling scared, they tell me to be brave.*

Boots slowly stepped out of the closet then quickly ran into Mrs. Meowington's arms. Holding him tightly, she asked if he was ready, then *VROOM!*

"IT'S JUST NOISE!" she yelled over the sound of the vacuum.

5
The Great Escape

Although he slept comfortably on blankets and was no longer afraid of dogs—or vacuums—something was missing.

Boots loved sitting on the Meowingtons' front window ledge, watching as the summer turned to fall and the fall turned to winter, but he missed being outside.

He smiled, remembering the fresh air on a beautiful junkyard morning, when he woke up in his work boot and began his morning hunt.

But now, with snow outside and the Meowingtons' windows closed tightly, the only fresh air Boots felt was when the front door opened for the dog's bathroom breaks.

That's when he got a sneaky idea.

I'll sneak outside when the Meowingtons open the front door. I'll take a quick walk while the dog goes to the bathroom, then sneak back inside when she's finished.

I'll be so quick—they'll never notice I was gone!

Each night, Boots watched out the window as the dog took one last bathroom break before bedtime. That's when he planned his great escape.

One winter night, when the light through the window turned dark, Boots waited near the front door and listened for the call.

"Time to go out, one last time!" Mr. Meowington announced to the dog.

Boots watched as the dog walked to the front door, where Mr. Meowington waited. When the dog arrived, Mr. Meowington turned the knob and opened the door.

Here we go! Boots thought as he leapt next to the dog, walking side-by-side through the open door, down the front stairs, and out into the fresh, winter air.

The dog turned left to find her spot in the yard, while Boots turned right to begin his quick, outdoor adventure.

I made it outside! he thought as he walked down the driveway. Boots admired his outdoor surroundings and took a deep breath of fresh air.

Being outside again made Boots feel like he was back in the junkyard, but it wasn't summer anymore! Boots shivered in the cold of winter.

Thank goodness I'll only be outside for a few minutes, he thought as he shivered again.

Feeling cold, Boots now missed his warm blankets. Oh, how he'd love to be back inside on the window ledge, taking a nap in the warm sun!

Time to head back inside, Boots thought as he turned to walk back.

Then he heard the front door *SLAM!*

6
Feeling Brave

"**O**H NO!" Boots yelled as he ran up the driveway toward the house.

It felt like only seconds passed since he escaped through the door. Now, he found himself sitting in the dark on the front stairs, staring at a closed door.

Is the dog already inside? he wondered.

Boots looked up at the window and locked eyes with his dog friend, who was staring back through the glass with her tongue hanging out.

His great escape didn't feel so great anymore!
Boots started to panic.

He knew the Meowingtons were already settled in their warm beds, and the door wouldn't open again until the dog's morning bathroom break. He shivered and knew he needed a plan, and he needed one fast.

Boots scampered down the stairs, walked around the snow-covered bushes, and slipped on a patch of ice. He fell flat on his belly!

When Boots tried to stand up, his white feet slipped in different directions, and down he went again!

This isn't a great escape—it's an awful escape!

Feeling cold and frustrated, Boots was ready to give up. Then he heard a strange noise:

"HOO-HOO! HOO-HOOOOO!"

Frightened, he looked toward the noise and saw a giant tree with bare branches. Boots saw it many times through the window, but now the tree looked darker and spookier than he remembered.

"HOO-HOO!" he heard again.

Boots squinted through the darkness and saw a stubby-looking bird. It was perched on a snowy branch, staring back at him with big, round eyes.

Don't be scared. It's just a bird, he thought, breathing slowly to calm himself. *I saw many birds in the junkyard.*

"HOO-HOO! HOO-HOOOOO!" the owl shouted louder.

Boots thought about running away. Then he got an idea. He slowly pushed himself off the ice and stood up on his feet.

Don't be a scaredy-cat, Boots told himself. *Be brave*!

Feeling confident, he pounced toward the tree.

The surprised owl flew from its branch into the dark, night sky. As he watched the owl, Boots remembered the little boy saying, "Being brave paid off!"

And so it did. Feeling proud but still shivering, Boots looked up and saw snowflakes falling from the sky. He needed to find a warm spot to rest until morning.

As he walked toward the house, he noticed a small hole in the lowest wooden board on the stairs. Boots laughed, remembering when he chased a mouse at the junkyard and how it escaped through a small hole.

Like the mouse, Boots pushed his body through the hole and settled in for a night under the stairs.

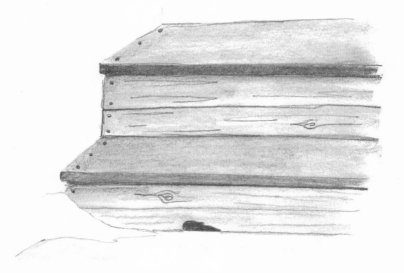

7
Don't Give Up

Boots woke up to another *SLAM!*

Once again, it was the Meowingtons' front door!

He was so tired after his escape from the house and his encounter with the owl that he slept through the dog's morning bathroom break. He missed his chance to go back inside!

Even worse, the overnight snow formed a pile next to the stairs, covering up the wooden board and the small hole.

Boots tried to push his body through the hole, but after seven attempts—and seven failures—he knew he was stuck under the front stairs where no one would find him.

He felt like giving up.

"BOOTS, WHERE ARE YOU?" Mrs. Meowington yelled from the front door.

She was searching for him! Boots felt happy, knowing Mrs. Meowington cared.

"Meow!" Boots answered.

"Boots, where are you?" she asked again, but this time it sounded quiet and far away from the stairs.

Boots gulped, then started to panic as his heart beat faster and faster in his chest.

She's going the wrong direction! She's walking away from me!

Boots felt cold, scared, and was almost ready to give up when he remembered the *BARK!* from the dog, the *VROOM!* from the vacuum, and the *HOO-HOOOOO!* from the owl.

Even though the loud noises made him feel scared, being brave paid off.

I can't be brave if I'm not afraid first, Boots realized.

I can't give up when I'm feeling scared.

I need to be brave!

"Meow! Meow!" Boots yelled, hoping she would answer, but there was no response.

Don't give up, he told himself. *Give it another try.*

"MEOW! MEOW!" Boots shouted as loud as he could.

"Boots? Is that you?" asked Mrs. Meowington. Her voice sounded louder and closer!

"MEOW!" Boots answered while celebrating. *Being brave paid off!*

And so it did. Mrs. Meowington ran toward the stairs, following his meows to the snow pile. Using her hands, she dug through the freezing, cold snow until she could see his gray hair and white feet.

"How did you get outside?" she asked Boots.

With snow now out of her way, Mrs. Meowington wiggled the wooden board until it felt loose. Then she pulled it off, finally freeing Boots from under the stairs. She lifted him from the ground and hugged him tightly.

"I can't wait to tell the family where I found you," Mrs. Meowington told Boots. "You're such a brave cat for finding a warm spot outside, but DON'T SNEAK OUT AGAIN!"

8
Families Belong Together

A few days passed since his great escape. Boots was now warm and comfortable inside, enjoying a nap on the sunny window ledge.

He was in the middle of a daydream when he woke to the sound of shrieking kids. He jumped down from the ledge to check out the excitement.

Boots noticed Mr. Meowington was home from work, and he put a brown cardboard box in the middle of the kitchen floor. Both the boy and girl were looking in the box.

What could it be?

From the high-pitched level of the shrieks, Boots thought it was a slithering snake. Or, maybe a mouse was in the house! Oh, how he'd love to chase a mouse again, just like when he hunted in the junkyard! He smiled at the memory but sighed when he thought of who he left behind: *Mama Cat.*

"A MAMA CAT!" the girl shrieked. "Can we keep her?"

Boots couldn't believe his ears. *Am I being replaced?*

While he thought about the news, Boots watched closely as Mr. Meowington lifted the cat from the box and tightly held her in his arms.

"Boots," he said directly, "I found your mom peeking in the junkyard office window!"

Mama Cat! Now Boots couldn't believe his ears OR his eyes!

"She must've been searching for you," Mr. Meowington continued. "The moment I saw her, I knew she was your mom. She was just as curious as you were, peeking in the window. And she looks just like you!"

Mr. Meowington put Mama Cat on the floor, giving the family its first look. Like Boots, she was gray from head-to-tail, with white hair on her chest and belly.

But one thing was different: she didn't have four white feet.

The little girl asked again, "Dad, can we keep her?"

Mr. Meowington answered quickly, "Families belong together. Boots is a member of this Meowington family, and so is his mom!"

The family laughed as Boots ran over to Mama Cat and rubbed his little face against hers.

Now that he was with his mom again, he no longer felt like something was missing. Boots felt happy, knowing they were both part of a big family.

"Let's give them some time to be together," Mrs. Meowington suggested. "They've been away from each other for too long."

9
Brave is Tough

"**Y**ou look bigger!" Mama Cat said as she circled around Boots. "You've grown so much!"

The mother and son were excited to be together again, and they spent the next few hours sharing stories.

Mama Cat shared how a gigantic bird stole his junkyard bed—the old, worn-out work boot.

They laughed when Boots shared his adventures with the barking dog, the vrooming vacuum, the hooting owl, and how he slept under the front stairs during his great escape.

Mama Cat looked pleased. "Dogs, vacuums, AND owls! Sounds like you were junkyard tough, just like I taught you," she said with pride.

"Oh Mama, I didn't feel tough," Boots said with an embarrassed tone. "Sure, I felt tough in the junkyard, but the loud noises at this house made me feel scared."

"It's OK to feel scared," Mama Cat said kindly. "How did you feel after you were scared?"

"Well, every time I felt afraid, the Meowingtons told me to be brave," he answered. "I realized I can't be brave if I'm not afraid first."

"That's right!" Mama Cat exclaimed. "But Boots, do you know what brave means?"

"Does it mean don't give up?" he asked. "Because I never gave up, Mama!"

Mama Cat sat quietly for a moment, deep in thought.

"Boots, what does junkyard tough mean?"

"That's easy!" he answered promptly. "It means I'm not a scaredy-cat!"

Mama Cat laughed at his answer.

"That's right! When you live in a junkyard, you need to be tough. The giant rats and noisy trucks in the junkyard never scared you, right?"

"No way! Because you taught me to be junkyard tough," he said.

"Boots, junkyard tough is how I taught you to be brave. Bravery is being tough, facing your fears, and never giving up—just like you did here with the dog, vacuum, and owl. Boots, you've always been brave, no matter where you've lived."

Boots stared at his mom, taking a moment to let her words sink in.

Bravery is junkyard tough!

Boots thought about his past adventures and realized no matter where he lived—in the junkyard or in the Meowingtons' house—he was a brave cat.

Bravery was always inside him.

With that realization, Boots leapt toward his mom and rubbed his little face against hers.

10
Family Picture

The sun already set, and a few hours passed since the family left the cats for their reunion.

Mrs. Meowington knew Mama Cat would be hungry—she hadn't eaten since she joined the family—so she poured a bowl full of cat food and gently placed it on the kitchen floor next to the water bowl.

"Have you checked on the cats?" Mrs. Meowington asked the kids.

"Nope, haven't seen them," the boy answered.

Now curious where the cats were, the kids began a search party through the Meowingtons' house.

Holding flashlights, they searched upstairs, explored downstairs, and hunted under beds. They even looked in the bathtub, but they didn't find the cats.

"Where are they?" the girl asked her brother. "Do you think they went outside, like when Boots slept under the stairs?"

Before the boy could answer, the girl opened the front door, stepped outside, and used her flashlight to look under the stairs. She didn't find the cats.

Meanwhile, the boy followed her outside and searched near the giant tree with bare branches. But like his sister, he didn't find the cats.

The search continued for an hour. Mr. Meowington and the dog joined the kids outside, asking neighbors if they saw Boots or Mama Cat. The search party was halfway down the street when Mrs. Meowington called them back inside.

"I noticed the closet door was slightly open," she told the family as they entered the house.

Everyone watched as she opened the closet door and revealed her discovery: Boots and Mama Cat were inside, sleeping side-by-side in Mr. Meowington's work boots!

That's when Mr. Meowington got an idea.

He snuck away with a smile on his face and returned with a camera in his hand.

"Everyone kneel down by the cats," he whispered. "Be careful not to wake them!"

He placed the camera on a table, set the timer, and joined the group, kneeling beside Mrs. Meowington and the dog. Everyone smiled when the camera flash clicked.

It was the perfect family picture for his frame at the junkyard office.

The group stood up and walked away, but Mr. Meowington stayed on the floor to pet Boots.

Boots opened his eyes and looked up at his old friend.

"Hey there, little buddy," Mr. Meowington said softly. "How about french fries for dinner?"

The End